WALTER
The Story of a Rat

Barbara Wersba

DRAWINGS BY
Donna Diamond

FRONT STREET
Asheville, North Carolina

This story is for Patricia S. Myrer
B.W.

For Swadesh Grant
D.D.

Copyright © 2005 by Barbara Wersba
Illustrations copyright © 2005 by Donna Diamond
All rights reserved
Printed in China
Designed by Helen Robinson
First edition

Library of Congress Cataloging-in-Publication Data
Wersba, Barbara.
Walter: the story of a rat / Barbara Wersba;
Donna Diamond, illustrator.—1st ed.
p. cm.
Summary: Walter, namesake of Sir Walter Scott
and a rat that can read, lives in the home of Miss Amanda
Pomeroy, a celebrated writer of children's books.
ISBN 1-932425-41-1 (alk. paper)
[1. Rats—Fiction. 2. Books and reading—Fiction. 3. Authors—Fiction.]
I. Diamond, Donna, ill. II. Title.
PZ7.W473Wal 2005
[Fic]—dc22
2005013369

FRONT STREET
A Division of Boyds Mills Press
A Highlights Company

WALTER
The Story of a Rat

Walter was a very old rat who lived with a writer named Amanda Pomeroy. Miss Pomeroy did not know that Walter lived with her—because he came out only at night—but of all the houses he had dwelled in, Walter liked Miss Pomeroy's the best. This was because she was a writer and owned hundreds of books.

For reasons he could not explain, Walter had been born with the ability to read. He had never known another rat who had this ability, but from the day he opened his eyes he was able to decipher printed words. When young, he had lived near the town dump and had read an entire pocket dictionary and two books by a man named Sir Walter Scott. Like most rats he didn't have a proper name, but that day he decided to christen himself Walter. Scott was obviously an important man because his books, though tattered, were bound in leather. Walter ate most of the leather, but left the pages intact.

Walter read whatever came his way—comic books, romance novels, and a book of essays by someone called Leonard Woolf. He had read a novel by Stephen King and three poems by Edna St. Vincent Millay. He had read the last act of a play by Tennessee Williams and a biography of Eleanor Roosevelt. The randomness of these choices was not his fault. He read whatever he could take from the dump, or from the library book sale, which was held outdoors in the spring.

Walter was a "Norway rat" or "Common rat," as the nature books described him. He preferred "Norway" to "Common," because he knew he was not common at all. Occasionally he chose to think of himself by his Latin name, which was *Rattus norvegicus.*

Walter was ten inches long and had gray-brown hair, lighter near the belly. His tail was thin and hairless and not his best feature, though it came in handy at times. His vocalizations included squeaks, whistles, and chirps, but—because he was so solitary—he rarely made a sound. The thing which had depressed him since childhood was the bad reputation his species suffered from. Sometimes after dinner, when Miss Pomeroy sat in the living room and watched TV, Walter would tiptoe out from his hiding place and sit quietly in a corner. Miss Pomeroy—he never thought of her as "Ms."—had a penchant for old movies, and it was not unusual to hear an actor on the screen say, "You dirty rat!" when referring to someone evil.

Once, years ago at the dump, Walter had rescued part of a book titled *A Field Guide to Small Mammals* and had read this about rats.

> *The Common rat is an insufferable nuisance. There is no courtesy or kindness in his nature; no nesting bird is safe from his attacks. He is a villain and will eat almost anything, from the refuse in the garbage heap to the dainty egg of a willow-wren. He is known to spread diseases such as typhus, spotted fever, and bubonic plague.*

The words had made Walter weep, for he himself—and most of his relatives—had always been kind, clean, and considerate. If they had spread diseases, they had been unaware of it—and as far as he could remember, he, Walter, had committed only one crime. In a moment of hunger and confusion he had eaten two of his offspring, but he had been only eight months old at the time—a young, impetuous rat—and he had never done it again.

Walter had lived in Miss Pomeroy's house for six months. Adjoining her kitchen was a storeroom, and behind an old bureau in this room was a hole in the floor. The hole led to a passageway

Walter had created, and leading from the passageway were several chambers. One chamber was for sleeping, and another for storing food. A third, larger chamber was his library, where he kept remnants of books and magazines. He usually read at night, though he had an unfortunate tendency to nibble the candles which gave him illumination.

At present Walter was reading a paperback book on Imperial Russia. Some very important people—royalty, actually—had been assassinated during a revolution long ago. Their dog, however, had been spared. It was a tragic tale filled with wonderful names—Nicholas, Alexandra, and Rasputin. Olga, Alexei, and Anastasia.

Words swam through Walter's mind like bright fish, darting back and forth. He did not always understand what he was reading, but the experience excited him. All those images, all those thoughts and ideas!

The first book he had owned was not exactly a book, but a book jacket—found in a trash can. The title on the jacket was *A Farewell to Arms*, and for a long time Walter had thought the story was about people losing their arms—a real predicament. How would they drive cars without arms? How would they cook dinner? A year later he had come across the book itself, and realized his mistake. *Arms* meant armaments. The book was about war.

There were many things Walter liked about Miss Pomeroy. The first was that she was old, like himself, and had streaks of white in her hair that resembled the white on his muzzle. And the second thing was that she was unconventional. She wrote her books not on a computer but on an old typewriter, and when she wrote she always wore a shabby blue bathrobe and stuck a pencil in her hair. She was careless in the kitchen, a habit that afforded him many midnight snacks, and often forgot to open her mail, which lay about on the hall table for days.

Whereas Miss Pomeroy was relentlessly untidy, Walter was neat. He kept the various chambers of his nest in perfect order, and was fussy about his appearance. Never a day passed when he did not groom his fur, clean his whiskers, and scrub his face with his front paws.

It was because of her mail—from agents and publishers—that Walter first realized Miss Pomeroy was a published writer. She wrote books for little children—"juveniles." She was famous! Miss Pomeroy, however, seemed not to care about fame. What she liked was to work at her rickety typewriter during the day and watch TV at night. She would drink white wine and talk out loud about the movies she watched, making comments. Her favorite film was *The Maltese Falcon*.

How miraculous, Walter thought, that he—a reader—had come to live in the house of a writer. It was a stroke of fate.

Because he was a sensitive creature, Walter understood that Miss Pomeroy was lonely. It was not that the world didn't want her—*she* didn't want the world. Perhaps "solitary" was a better word than lonely, but no one ever came to the house and—thank goodness—she did not own a cat. She slept late every morning and drank black coffee for breakfast. She snacked rather than preparing real meals, and sometimes lay flat on the floor, listening to music. There were no family photographs in her bedroom, and she never made her bed. Her phone rarely rang.

One of the reasons all this interested Walter was that he was lonely himself. Rats have short lives, but he had lived on and on—the white in his muzzle a little more pronounced each year, his joints growing stiffer. He could no longer remember his parents, his siblings, or his many mates. Everyone was gone.

"To be or not to be," Walter often said to himself. "That is the question." The words had been written by a poet named Shakespeare. A drawing of him was on display in the municipal building, and Walter had often admired his face. He was bald, but had lovely eyes.

Did Miss Pomeroy write poetry, he wondered? He had yet to find the books she had published—in her library, on the second floor—because the library was so disorganized. Books on theater sat next to books on fish and snails. Biographies were mixed in with murder mysteries. A book on New Zealand sat alongside two volumes of Sigmund Freud.

Every night, after Miss Pomeroy retired, Walter would scamper upstairs to borrow a book, which he always returned in the morning. He was trying to read his way through the entire room—no mean feat, as Miss Pomeroy owned hundreds of books, some of them new, but most of them quite tattered and old. One volume, called *You Can't Go Home Again*, had always attracted Walter and he intended to read it soon. The title moved him to tears, for he himself had never been able to return to his first home—a laundromat which had burnt to the ground. Sometimes, in dreams, he could recapture the pungent smell of the place and recall the wonderful things he had eaten there—fragments of candy bars and discarded bags of potato chips. Small boxes of Ivory Flakes. His nest had been under the floorboards, and he had found the steady hum of the washing machines strangely soothing.

How many places he had lived! The laundromat, the municipal building, two houses on Main Street, three trash heaps. He had had so many adventures—but most of them were fading from his mind, like old movies, and at times he wondered if his life held any meaning at all.

"I am past my prime," Walter thought. "Long past it." It was, of course, a phrase he had found in a book.

T he town where Walter lived was a small one called Safe Harbor. There was a main street with shops, a few side streets with houses, and that was all. There was a movie house and a municipal building, an antique store and an Italian restaurant. At the end of Main Street was a pier where boats tied up in the summer—and beyond the pier was an expanse of water called Hammond's Bay. Walter knew the town like the back of his paw. He could have navigated it blindfolded.

He could not recall where he had been born, but by the time he was a few weeks old he was living with his siblings beneath the laundromat. His mother, whom he could barely remember, had been a busy creature—rushing back and forth with food for her family. She had brought them squashed fruit from the Dumpster behind the grocery store. She had brought them lovely morsels of bread and cookies.

Then one day she was gone—and it was not long before Walter's siblings were gone too. Off to fend for themselves. Off to wander, and breed, and face a hundred dangers. Off to die at the hand of some cruel human who was afraid of rats.

That was the problem—the human species' fear of rats. From the time he was an adolescent, humans had thrown stones at Walter, shot guns at him, and repeatedly tried to poison him with some strange-smelling food, which he had been wise enough to avoid. They had kicked at him, screamed at him, and once—at the very sight of him—a young woman had fainted. Walter had never been able to understand the horror he and his relatives aroused in humans. These, after all, were the same people who kept hamsters and guinea pigs as pets. The same children who loved white mice. These

were the people who fed squirrels in the park and walked tiny dogs on leashes. As far as Walter was concerned, animals were animals—all of them equally important.

The only place Walter had ever lived where he was not persecuted was Miss Pomeroy's house—but that was because Miss Pomeroy did not know he was there. He was very careful to come out of his nest only at night, and never left droppings around—a habit he disapproved of. He rarely took more food from Miss Pomeroy's kitchen than he needed, and never uttered so much as a squeak. As far as he himself was concerned, Walter was a good rat—clean, neat, and thoughtful.

Miss Pomeroy's house was one block from the pier that extended into Hammond's Bay—and sometimes, at twilight, she would put on an old straw hat and stroll along the pier. Walter would watch from a distance, strangely moved by her awkward gait and old-fashioned clothes—moved by her shyness, which was so very apparent. If a passerby said "Good evening" to her, she would nod curtly and keep on walking. She never chatted with anyone, and she spent little money. Walter had never seen her buy an ice-cream cone.

At the end of the pier Miss Pomeroy would sit down on a bench. Sometimes she brought stale bread with her, for the sea gulls. She would stare straight ahead, at the boats and the water. She would watch the slow sinking of the sun—an orange globe on the

horizon. Then she would rise and walk home, and if these excursions gave her any pleasure, she did not show it. What a strange person she was, Walter thought. Had she ever been happy?

Miss Pomeroy's house was as strange as she was—plain, untidy, and uncared for—except for the library on the second floor. *This* room she swept and dusted once a week, as though she was doing it for the sake of the books, and it was here that she lay on the floor and listened to music. She had a fine CD player, one of the few modern objects in the house, and she seemed to prefer Mozart to all other composers. Sometimes, while lying on the floor, she would wave her hand in the air, as though she was conducting the orchestra.

Walter felt the loneliness inside Miss Pomeroy as keenly as his own loneliness—but he did not know what to do about it. His fear was that once she saw him she would react like all the other humans he had known—with revulsion. He could not bear the thought that she might faint. He could not bear the idea that she might rush out to buy rat poison.

When he had first moved into Miss Pomeroy's house he had tentatively considered making friends with her—and had picked a daisy in the yard and left it on the hall table. She had not responded to this gesture of friendship. Then he had left her part of an article from a magazine called *The New Yorker*. It was about famous writers who had once lived in Paris, France.

Miss Pomeroy had noticed the article, had put on her glasses and skimmed it, and then tossed it aside. After those two overtures, Walter had given up.

Rats are social animals, but Walter did not have any rat friends. People in the town were so hostile toward rodents that most of the local rats stayed in hiding. Once, on the pier where Miss Pomeroy took her walks, he had come face to face with a ship's rat who had sailed in on an antique schooner—a rented one, used to attract tourists—but this rat had shrieked and run away at the sight of Walter, not recognizing him as a comrade.

Walter knew that there were Black rats and Brown rats, White rats—used, alas, in laboratories—and something called Pack rats. He knew there were Bandicoot rats and Muskrats,

and also Kangaroo rats. But if any of these creatures lived in Safe Harbor, he was unaware of them.

One of the few bits of advice Walter's mother had given him—before she disappeared—was always to be "positive and hopeful." Thus, Walter still hoped to have a friend someday. "Hope is the thing with feathers that perches in the soul," he said to himself. He liked this quotation—first because it mentioned feathers, and second because of its optimism. On the other hand, he thought, things with feathers often fly away.

Walter was slowly working his way through Miss Pomeroy's library. He had read parts of *The Way of All Flesh*—which was an unpleasant title—and all of *Franny and Zooey*. He had read the end of a romance novel called *This Raging Desire*, and a book about penguins. At present he was reading a play called *The Little Foxes*, which was turning out to be a disappointment, as there was not a single fox in it.

Entering the library each night around eleven—when Miss Pomeroy was asleep—Walter would explore the bookshelves. Rats are not good climbers, but Miss Pomeroy had a ladder which helped her reach the highest shelves, and Walter found the ladder invaluable. He would scamper over yards and yards of books, picking titles at random.

He would never forget the day he learned to read—or rather, the day when reading happened to him. It was not a question of learning, it was a matter of instant comprehension. One moment he had been dozing in his nest beneath the laundromat—pressed up against his siblings, feeling warm and contented—and the next moment his eyes had fastened upon some torn pages his mother had used for the nest lining. The markings on one page slowly formed themselves into letters—the letters into words—and suddenly these words had meaning. Walter still remembered the exact words, because he found them beautiful.

And as I sat there brooding on the old, unknown world, I thought of Gatsby's wonder when he first picked out the green light at the end of Daisy's dock. He had come a long way to this blue lawn, and his dream must have seemed so close that he could hardly fail to grasp it. He did not know that it was already behind him, somewhere back in that vast obscurity beyond the city, where the dark fields of the republic rolled on under the night.

He would never know who Gatsby was, or Daisy, or why Gatsby's dream was behind him, but the words had caused a terrible excitement inside Walter, almost greater than the excitement he felt when his mother brought food into the nest. There was no word for such excitement. It was related, somehow, to *adventure.*

One night Walter was scampering over a section in Miss Pomeroy's library that he had never investigated before—a curious section which held books both large and small. The large books had colored illustrations and few words, while the smaller books seemed to concentrate more upon stories. With the insight that Walter prided himself on, he realized that these were children's books, the kind Miss Pomeroy wrote!

Surprisingly, the authors of these books were in alphabetical order, and it was not long before he found the letter P. "P for Pomeroy," he said to himself, and sure enough, there were her published works—all twenty of them.

It was then that Walter received a shock—one that almost made him lose his footing and fall to the floor—for Miss Pomeroy's books were all about mice. Not factual books about mice, but fanciful ones. Fantasies. The hero was a mouse named Bromberg.

Bromberg Goes to Moscow read one title. *Bromberg and the Hidden Door* read another. It went on and on—endless stories about Bromberg who, it turned out, was a secret-agent mouse working for the government. And not only was Bromberg a mouse, everyone else in the stories were mice as well. Mice detectives and mice spies. Mice villains and mice heroes. Elderly mice, who were always in some kind of danger. Rich female mice, kidnapped and held for ransom.

Walter sat on Miss Pomeroy's ladder studying these books, and he did not know whether to laugh or cry. He felt betrayed—for why had Miss Pomeroy chosen to write about mice when she could just as easily have chosen rats? How could she not have known that rats are more interesting than mice, more intelligent, and more adaptable? To put it bluntly, how could she not have known that rats are more magnificent?

Walter returned the books to their place on the shelf. Then, with a certain foreboding, he began to study the entire children's book section. What he found amazed him—for not only did Miss Pomeroy write books about mice, lots of others did too. There was a mouse hero named Stuart Little, and one named Noisy Nora. There was a dancing mouse called Angelina, and a watchmaker mouse called Hermux. There was a mouse named Abel who was marooned on an island. There was a whole *flock* of little books by a woman named Potter, which dealt obsessively with mice. Mice in vests and trousers, mice with parasols. What did it mean?

It was all too clear what it meant. Human people hated rats, so they wrote about mice. Humans found rats ugly and mice adorable. Rats were large and mice were small. Mice were not known to spread diseases.

With a heavy heart, Walter borrowed *Bromberg Goes to Moscow* and took it downstairs to his nest. By the flickering light of a scented candle—one he had found in the garbage—he studied Miss Pomeroy's creation. It was not that the book was badly written—on the contrary, it was interesting. Written long ago, it concerned something called the "cold war." Bromberg the secret-agent mouse was on a mission for the Pentagon. He had stowed away on a Russian airliner in order to find some special papers in a government office in Moscow. His mission was to find the papers and eat them, so that the world would be spared an unnamed catastrophe.

The book was illustrated with black-and-white pictures by a man named Samuel Slater. On the back of the jacket were brief biographies of this Slater person and Miss Pomeroy. Amanda Pomeroy, the jacket said, had been writing children's books for the past thirty years and had won many honors and awards. She lived in a small town in New York State, and her hobbies were cooking and gardening.

"Cooking and gardening!" Walter said aloud. How totally dishonest. Miss Pomeroy neither cooked nor gardened. Like himself, she existed on sandwiches and snacks, and her backyard was a jungle. As for Samuel Slater, the jacket said that he was a well-known illustrator who had once lived in Africa, in order to draw and photograph wild animals—but who knew if this was true?

Walter tried to finish *Bromberg Goes to Moscow* before his candle gave out. "My candle burns at both ends," he murmured. "It will not last the night." This was not actually true, for Walter had never had a candle that behaved that way—but the quotation gave him comfort. The disappointment he felt in Miss Pomeroy was so palpable he could almost taste it. It was a bitter taste, like a chocolate truffle he had once saved for a year, which had spoiled.

As his scented candle began to wane and flicker, Walter fell asleep.

He woke the next morning determined to have a showdown with Miss Pomeroy. Gone were his feelings of concern and sympathy—and in their place were feelings that were quite uncharitable. If he had taken a moment to search his soul, Walter would have realized that his disappointment in Miss Pomeroy was connected to his admiration for her. He did not, however, take the time to consider this. Instead, he tried to decide how best to make contact with her. "A letter," he said to himself. "I will borrow a piece of stationery from her office and write her a letter."

This posed a problem—for the only letter Walter had ever written in his life was a letter of condolence to a cousin who had lost a litter of babies in a toilet-bowl accident. It was a superfluous letter, since his cousin could not read, but he had felt strongly about her loss and had left the letter in her nest anyway. As far as he could remember, it had said,

> *You may not remember me, but we are cousins. Our mothers, who lived near the dump, were sisters and very fond of each other. At any rate, I wish to express my sadness at the loss of your six babies, who could not swim. Had they lived longer, I am sure they would have learned how.*
> *Sincerely,*
> *Your first cousin, Walter*

What should he say to Miss Pomeroy? It would be crude to come right out and express his disgust over her *oeuvre* of mouse books.

What he should probably do was leave her a brief message—one that would establish some contact, if not rapport, between them. Thus, late that night Walter scurried up to Miss Pomeroy's office, which was across the hall from her library.

This little office was as messy as the other rooms in the house. There was a desk, a lamp, an easy chair, and a bulging file cabinet. There were discarded pieces of typing paper all over the floor. An ancient teddy bear sat in the waste- basket.

On top of Miss Pomeroy's desk was a box of blue stationery, and Walter decided to use this for his message. Carefully, he chose a ballpoint pen from a jar of pens on the windowsill. Carefully, he flicked on the desk lamp. Then he settled himself in the easy chair and pondered what to say. Should he say, "I am a rat-in-residence here and have just examined your collection of children's books. I am sorry to have to tell you that . . ."

No, that wouldn't do at all. It sounded pompous. What about "I am a local rat who has chosen to share this house with you, and I have recently had the opportunity to study your terrible collection of books."

That too was wrong. Rude and unkind. My goodness, he thought, it was hard to write words! Walter had never known this before, and it impressed him. Why was it easy to read words, but hard to write them? Maybe it was because there were so many words to choose from.

After two hours of sitting in Miss Pomeroy's easy chair and nibbling the tip of her ballpoint pen, Walter wrote his letter to Miss Pomeroy. It was very brief. It said,

My name is Walter.
I live here too.

He left the letter on top of her typewriter, where she would be most likely to see it. And, as an afterthought, he signed it with the drawing of a paw print. That way, she might guess he was a rodent.

Walter slept most of the next day. After leaving his letter for Miss Pomeroy he had raided her kitchen and found an open can of cashew nuts, half an apple, and two Bath biscuits. He had also sampled a glass of white wine she had left on top of the television set. He had not liked the wine at all, and it made him so sleepy that he slept till afternoon, snug in his bed of old socks and autumn leaves. He woke thinking of the words he had written to Miss Pomeroy, and the memory of them filled him with dread. What a presumptuous thing to have done! What would the repercussions be?

The house was very quiet. No sound of Miss Pomeroy in the kitchen. No sound of her upstairs, typing. And since the weather was mild, Walter decided to sit in the backyard for a while. He always did this at his peril, as Miss Pomeroy's neighbor owned a dog.

Walter's nest had one entrance, but three exits—to be used in cases of emergency—and the farthest exit led to the backyard. Yawning, he strolled out into the late-day sunshine. It was October, and a soft blue haze filled the sky, mingled with the smell of burning leaves. What a pity that Miss Pomeroy was *not* a gardener. Her backyard was a tangle of daisies and roses and weeds. There was a stone statue, a stone bench, and a fence that was falling down. There were red berries on some of the bushes.

Walter settled down on Miss Pomeroy's bench and perused the world. It was very beautiful, and he longed to have someone to share it with. He would liked to have said, to someone, "Aren't those roses amazing?" And then this person would reply, "Walter, you are correct. Those are the best roses I have ever seen."

"Ah, but it's autumn," Walter said to his imaginary friend. "The roses will soon be gone."

"A thing of beauty is a joy forever," the imaginary friend replied. "Take my word for it."

Why had the book jacket lied about Miss Pomeroy being a gardener? And a cook! The only things she ever put in the oven were frozen dinners, the remnants of which Walter never liked. And why did she keep a teddy bear in the wastebasket?

Walter spent an hour in the garden. Then he returned to his nest and settled down to read. He had dragged a book called *The Heart Is a Lonely Hunter* downstairs, as the title suited his mood.

Walter waited till midnight. Very quietly, he tiptoed upstairs to see if Miss Pomeroy had received his letter. She had probably glanced at it in disgust and tossed it away. It was possible that she had not even seen it. His whiskers trembling with excitement, Walter entered Miss Pomeroy's office, jumped up on the desk, and looked for his letter, which had said,

> *My name is Walter.*
> *I live here too.*

His letter was gone. And in its place, on top of the typewriter, was a reply in Miss Pomeroy's handwriting. The reply said,

> *I know.*

It was a very short reply. Still, Miss Pomeroy had written it to him, and Walter cherished it. He went downstairs to his nest and put her letter in a prominent place, next to a pile of paperback books and a picture postcard of Abraham Lincoln. He had found the postcard tucked into a history book long ago, and had decided to keep it.

The incredible thing was that Miss Pomeroy knew of his existence. How amazing that was! For months he had been tiptoeing around the house, appearing only at night, hiding in corners while she watched television . . . when all along she had known he was there. What did it portend? She had not tried to shoot him or poison him. She had not thrown stones at him, and he had never once seen her faint. Did this mean that she accepted his presence? Or did it simply mean she was indifferent?

Walter stared at Miss Pomeroy's letter. "I know," it said. Only two words—but they filled him with emotion.

Walter decided to write another letter to Miss Pomeroy. A longer one this time, and one that was not critical of her mouse-oriented books. The purpose of this second letter would be to make friends with Miss Pomeroy, to start a dialogue between them.

By now it was two in the morning. Once again, Walter sat in Miss Pomeroy's easy chair, nibbling on one of her ballpoint pens. He had a piece of blue stationery on his lap, with a book under it to serve as a writing-board. A soft rain was falling outside.

Dear Miss Pomeroy, Thank you for writing me. Your letter was short, but I loved it. My name, as I said before, is Walter, and my Latin name is Rattus norvegicus. *I have lived here for six months and have no friends. No relatives, either. I am reading all of your books and hope you don't mind. I always return them to their places.*
   Sincerely,
   Walter (named after Sir Walter Scott)

Walter put his new letter on top of Miss Pomeroy's typewriter. Then he returned to his nest and slept for ten hours. His dreams were troubled, and several times he woke with a squeak, trying to shake off the strange images which were haunting him. In one dream, Miss Pomeroy had turned into the ship's rat he had seen on the pier. It was her face, but on a rat's body. In another dream, she had become very small and was trying to move into his nest. Finally, around noon of the next day, he had a pleasant dream. He and Miss Pomeroy were sitting in the garden, on the stone bench, discussing roses.

Walter waited until eleven that night, when Miss Pomeroy was asleep. Once again, he headed upstairs to her office. Sure enough, she had left a letter for him—a longer one, written in a strangely elegant handwriting. "Dear Walter," the letter began.

Dear Walter: I am not exactly a fool. I saw you the very day you moved in, six months ago. I know where your nest is, and I know you steal food from my kitchen. My Latin name is Homo sapiens, *and I am well aware that you are reading my books. You presume a great deal! On the other hand, you are not unwelcome here.*

Amanda Pomeroy

Walter read the letter three times. It was hard to understand its true meaning, for it seemed both hostile and friendly. This was what people meant by a *paradox*, but he, Walter, had never been good at paradoxes. There were several harsh things in the letter, such as, "I know you steal food from my kitchen." On the other hand, Miss Pomeroy had also said, "You are not unwelcome here."

Walter decided to write a third letter—only this time he would leave a little gift with it. The one interesting thing he owned was the picture postcard of Abraham Lincoln, so he decided to leave that as a peace offering. His third letter said,

Dear Miss Pomeroy, I am excited to be in touch with you, and wonder if we could share our thoughts and ideas. Your books about mice interest me. Could we ever discuss them? I never felt that I was "stealing" from you.

Do forgive me. I am leaving you a present. A picture postcard.
    Walter

Miss Pomeroy's reply was waiting for him the following night.

   Walter: I am willing to share some thoughts and ideas with you, and if the word "stealing" offends you, then I'm sorry. But please, do not eat the English biscuits, as they are expensive. Another thing: stop chewing on my pens.
    I like the picture of Lincoln.
    Amanda Pomeroy

For the next three weeks Walter and Miss Pomeroy wrote each other frequently. They discussed the weather, the state of Miss Pomeroy's library, and the location of Walter's nest. Miss Pomeroy was not pleased that Walter's nest had an exit that opened into the garden, but Walter explained that he was a vigilant rat and would not allow other creatures to enter the house.

Shyly, Walter asked Miss Pomeroy why her book jackets

proclaimed her a gardener and a cook. Irritably, Miss Pomeroy replied that she *had* been a gardener and a cook—long ago, when she was young. Then Walter committed a *faux pas*. He asked Miss Pomeroy why she wrote books for little children.

Her reply was swift and rather angry.

I write for children because I do not particularly like grownups.

The weather was colder now, and for her walks along the pier Miss Pomeroy wore an old felt hat instead of her summer straw one. Sometimes she took a walking stick with her, and would

swipe at things which got in her way. She always brought stale bread for the sea gulls, however, and always sat on the same bench, staring at the sunset. Walter would follow at a distance—strangely moved by the sight of her. He would crouch behind a piling, trying to share Miss Pomeroy's feelings about the sunset. When she turned to walk home, he would trail behind.

Miss Pomeroy always read in bed for an hour before falling asleep, and, very carefully, Walter began to join her in the bedroom. Tiptoeing into a far corner with a paperback book, he would read while she read, and stop when she stopped. Miss Pomeroy was absorbed in a biography of Mozart. He, Walter, was trying to finish a book of short stories called *The Little Disturbances of Man*.

Humans suffered from many disturbances, Walter thought. Love, sorrow, poverty, and loneliness. But life was not so different for rats. He himself had known sorrow—and loneliness was a constant in his life. What were Miss Pomeroy's disturbances, he wondered. Most of all, why was she so angry all the time?

Miss Pomeroy came in contact with very few people, but those few irritated her. Greeting the delivery boy who brought groceries twice a week, she would say, "How many times do I have to tell you this? I ordered tangerines, not oranges! And last week the milk was sour!" Talking on the phone to a mysterious person called an "agent," Miss Pomeroy would sputter, "I cannot be pushed, Miss Thompson! The book will be finished when it's finished. Let *me* call *you* next time."

Walter wondered if the human condition was destined to make humans angry. He wondered why humans went to war. Then he began to wonder if Miss Pomeroy had ever had friends or relatives—or even a spouse. So very few things gave her pleasure. She never went shopping.

She was, however, writing a new book about Bromberg, the secret-agent mouse. Every night, when Walter scurried upstairs, he would find discarded typewriter pages on the floor of her office. This time, Bromberg was in the Middle East, trying to foil a terrorist plot. He had become involved with an exotic mouse named Jasmine.

Walter's goal was to read all twenty of the Bromberg books. The more of them he read, the more he began to understand what Miss Pomeroy was doing. The books were not shallow, as he once had thought. Instead, they used animals to reveal things about *people*. What was this called, he wondered. Allergy? No, allegory.

There was only one person Miss Pomeroy seemed able to tolerate—and that was Samuel Slater, who illustrated her books. Whenever *he* phoned, from some distant place, her voice would soften a little. "Yes," she would say quietly, "I know that." "Yes, Sammy, I quite agree with you."

Walter invented a fantasy about Samuel Slater being in love with Miss Pomeroy. Rats, of course, never "fell in love"—they mated—but humans seemed to do this frequently. Falling in love was an expression that denoted pain, Walter thought. Like the time he had fallen into a bucket at the laundromat and injured his paw.

Feeling a bit guilty, Walter hurried around Miss Pomeroy's office, looking for letters from Samuel Slater. There were none. Then he began to study the mail, which lay unopened on the hall table. Only once did he find a postcard from Samuel— from Paris—and it showed a bookstore called Shakespeare and Company. The message said, "Jessica and I are spending a fortune here. Dozens and dozens of great books. Wish you were with us. (signed) Sammy."

So . . . Samuel had a wife, or mate, named Jessica. He was

not in love with Miss Pomeroy at all. Walter studied the picture on the postcard. It showed a very crowded bookstore, and this message was printed at the top.

Be not inhospitable to strangers,
lest they be angels in disguise.

Thanksgiving week came and went without a celebration. Walter knew that most humans celebrated this holiday because the local newspaper—which Miss Pomeroy had delivered to the house—kept talking about it. The Italian restaurant on Main Street would be having a "Thanksgiving Special." There was going to be a "Thanksgiving Day Parade" sponsored by the high school. People ate turkeys, unfortunately, on Thanksgiving, and stayed home with their families.

"Happy families are all alike," Walter said to himself. "Every unhappy family is unhappy in its own way." This was one of the quotations he had stored in his brain, but he could not remember what book it had come from. All he could remember was that the book was too heavy to be dragged downstairs and that he had read parts of it in Miss Pomeroy's library.

What a pity that he and Miss Pomeroy were not a family. What a pity she showed no interest in meeting him.

Their letters, however, were continuing—and rare was the day when Miss Pomeroy did not inform him of *something*. She was very bossy, and loved to give instructions. It was thoughtful of him, she said, to no longer eat the Bath biscuits, but would he please not leave cherry pits on the floor. Also, she was missing a pair of white cotton socks and wondered if he, Walter, had taken them.

Walter felt ashamed—for he had indeed taken the socks, for his nest. He returned them to Miss Pomeroy's closet immediately.

The weather was cold now, and on Thanksgiving Day a few snowflakes fluttered into the yard. Walter lined his sleeping chamber with a towel he had found in the trash, and continued to save the candle stubs Miss Pomeroy was always throwing away. It was hard for him to decide whether he was borrowing things from her or stealing them, but he did have certain needs—the greatest of these being food and warmth. To his delight, Miss Pomeroy threw away a rusty pocket watch which still worked. Walter put it near his bed and enjoyed the gentle ticking sound.

Walter and Miss Pomeroy had been in touch, so to speak, for weeks—and a terrible need was growing inside him to share his feelings about the subject of rats versus mice. It would take courage to bring this subject into the open, but he did not feel their relationship could continue without some kind of understanding. Children's books were filled with mice, but had a paucity of rats. It was deeply unfair.

One Sunday night, around eleven, Walter sat in Miss Pomeroy's easy chair composing a letter. Trying not to nibble on one of her ballpoint pens, he wrote,

> *Dear Miss Pomeroy, I have enjoyed our correspondence so much, but I want to ask you something. I hope it will not make you angry. What I want to ask you is this. Why do you write only about mice, and never rats? Why does everyone else do this too? Those of us who are rats feel hurt. Please do not take this as a criticism.*
> *Walter*

Miss Pomeroy replied the following night.

> *Dear Walter: You have a point. Most people would rather write about mice than rats. And yet, the rat has a real history in literature! There is the story of "The Pied Piper of Hamelin," in which all the rats, unfortunately,*

are led away to their doom. But there is also a classic called The Wind in the Willows *in which a rat features both prominently and positively. Oscar Wilde mentions a rat in a fairy tale called* The Devoted Friend, *and there is an interesting rat in the Harry Potter books. Finally, there is a charming children's book called* The Boy, the Rat, and the Butterfly, *which I recommend to you. It is in my library, in the children's section, under* R *for Regniers, the author's name.*

In haste, Amanda Pomeroy

Walter was stunned. Not only was this the longest letter Miss Pomeroy had ever written him, it was also the friendliest. Not once did it scold or instruct him. Not once did it have overtones that were hostile. Miss Pomeroy obviously enjoyed talking about literature, and it was clear that—in this area, at least—she did not find him inferior. With great excitement, Walter hurried into Miss Pomeroy's library and dragged *The Wind in the Willows* down from a high shelf.

The book was too large for him to take to his nest, so he read parts of it right there—sitting by the window, in the moonlight. It was true! The rat in this story was presented very positively. He was even witty at times.

"Who is Kenneth Grahame?" Walter wrote to Miss Pomeroy.

"Did he invent graham crackers?" With some exasperation, Miss Pomeroy replied that crackers were *not* connected with this particular author, who lived a most unhappy life and died in 1932.

Walter kept himself busy the following week by reading all the things Miss Pomeroy had recommended. He read *The Devoted Friend* by Oscar Wilde. He finished *The Wind in the Willows*. He read *The Boy, the Rat, and the Butterfly*, in which the rat is an educated creature who recites poetry. Then he delved further into the world of children's books.

There was an English lady named Poppins who could slide up banisters—an incredible feat, Walter thought—and a frog who turned into a prince. There was an emperor who believed he was well-clothed when he was really naked, and a wizard from a place called Oz who turned out to be a "humbug"—which Walter envisioned as a large moth.

Nothing in these stories was what it seemed to be! And the sadness in them affected Walter deeply. A tin soldier, who loved a little dancer made of paper, burned up in a fire. A young fir tree, who thought he had an important future, became a Christmas tree and was then discarded. The Babes in the Wood actually *died*. Of starvation.

Were all children's stories filled with tragedy, Walter asked himself. No wonder Miss Pomeroy wrote about Bromberg, the secret-agent mouse who always triumphed in the end.

Suddenly, Walter was aware of all the things he did not know. There were hundreds—thousands—of books in the world, and he had read only a handful of them. One day he would die, a myriad of books unread, his knowledge of the world incomplete. This thought saddened him so much that he retreated to his nest and stayed there for two days, dozing fitfully and listening to the ticking of Miss Pomeroy's pocket watch.

Once again, his dreams were troubled. He dreamed that an entire shelf of books in the library fell on top of him. He dreamed that his tail was caught between the covers of an encyclopedia. At last he dreamed of a sunny day in the garden. He, Miss Pomeroy, and the neighbor's dog were all having a picnic together. In this dream, the dog was friendly.

Walter wrote a brief letter to Miss Pomeroy.

> *Dear Miss Pomeroy, I am saddened by the things I do not know. There are hundreds—thousands—of books in the world and I will never be able to read all of them. I am old.*
> *Walter*

Miss Pomeroy replied promptly.

> *Walter: I understand how you feel. But why the self-*

pity? I am old too, and ignorant, and yet I do my best. It
is all a person—or a rat—can do.
*   Amanda*

She had signed it "Amanda." And what's more, she had called herself ignorant. Ignorant! thought Walter. Why, she is the smartest human I have ever known—and also the humblest.

Dear Miss Pomeroy, (Walter wrote late that night) I
hope I am not being too forward, but I want you to know
that I admire you. You are a famous writer and yet you
disdain the things of this world. You work hard during
the day and do nothing at night but watch a little TV.
You are not a spendthrift. These are things I admire.
*   Walter*

After a few days, Miss Pomeroy replied.

Well, Walter, those are very nice compliments. I'm
not certain that I deserve them, but the words are good
to hear. You are special too—though you don't know
it—and I think you have a benevolent view of the world.
Not everyone does, believe me.
*   Amanda*

December came with drifting snowflakes and cold nights. The pier was empty now—there were no boats or tourists—and Miss Pomeroy took her walks wearing an old tweed overcoat. Things in the household were as they had always been, with one strange difference. Miss Pomeroy was beginning to tidy up. The first Walter had seen of this was when she gathered all the stray magazines and newspapers and put them in the trash. Next, she pulled an old vacuum cleaner out of the closet and vacuumed the living room. She tied her hair up in a scarf and hummed a bit as she dusted the bedroom. She began to organize the library.

Walter was amazed by her behavior, for as long as he had known Miss Pomeroy she had made a point of being disorganized. She had hired a cleaning woman only once—and promptly fired her—and she had never been willing to cope with the garden. It was a sorry sight, with all the flowers dead and the weeds straggly and brown—but here, too, she was beginning to make changes. At noontime, when the sun was warm, she would stride into the backyard with clippers and a rake. Furiously, she would attack the weeds and the brown flower stalks. One day she even brought out a hammer and tried to repair the fence.

Some individuals—like Walter—accumulate things. Others, like Miss Pomeroy, take a certain pleasure in throwing things out. Thus it was that Miss Pomeroy threw out a number of objects during this period. She threw out a set of reference books

on tropical diseases, and an old, battered globe of the world. She threw out three pairs of tennis shoes and five T-shirts. She also discarded a very curious object—a tarnished silver locket. Walter rescued the locket and took it back to his nest. There was a message engraved on the inside that baffled him. It said, "The course of true love never did run smooth. Forgive me. S."

Walter did not want to make too much of Miss Pomeroy's new behavior, but at the same time he wanted to mention it. He wrote,

*Dear Miss Pomeroy, The house and garden are begin-
ning to look very nice. Quite neat, really. Do you ever
celebrate Christmas?*

Her reply came quickly.

*Walter: My mother used to say that cleanliness is next
to godliness, and I suppose she was right. I have not celebrated Christmas for twenty years. Do you* care *about
Christmas?*

Walter wrote his reply in a single word.

Yes.

A week before Christmas, the town of Safe Harbor took
on a festive air. Colored lights were strung up and down
Main Street, and all the shop windows had decorations in them.
At the end of the pier stood a large Christmas tree. The man who
ran the drugstore dressed up as Santa Claus.

Walter knew about Christmas because one of the houses he

had lived in had five children in the family, and the parents of this noisy group were generous people. Not only was there a Christmas tree in the living room, but one in the dining room as well. There were piles of presents, and Christmas parties, and, of all things, a hired clown. The house rang with laughter and good cheer for many days, and Walter, from his hiding place—a hole in the wall—had watched the festivities.

Now Christmas was coming again, but Miss Pomeroy seemed oblivious of it. She was deep in her new book about Bromberg, and sometimes she worked until dinnertime. The Christmas cards she received lay in a pile on the hall table. The refrigerator was bare.

Feeling his usual guilt, Walter read some of Miss Pomeroy's Christmas cards. There were two from Samuel Slater, in Paris, and a large expensive-looking one from Miss Thompson, the "agent." There was a card signed "Hilary."
There was a box of candy canes from the grocery store.

A plant arrived from the florist, a lovely one with red flowers on it. The card read, "Thinking of you during the holidays and sending much love. The Wilsons." A crate of oranges arrived from Florida.

Rather than cheering Walter, these signs of Christmas depressed him. It would have been different if Miss Pomeroy had put up a tree, or wrapped some presents, but she was too misanthropic. "Misanthropic" was the latest word Walter had discovered, and it suited the situation perfectly.

The correspondence between Walter and Miss Pomeroy had waned a little—probably because she was so busy with her book. He had written her a brief letter, wishing her "Happy Holidays." She had written back, wishing him the same. But it was all rather tame.

On the other hand, Walter thought, Miss Pomeroy seemed to have no relatives—and had she had some, she might have behaved differently. A grandchild or two, a cheerful brother who smoked a pipe, a cousin visiting for the holidays . . . such people might have made a difference. Walter tried to imagine Miss Pomeroy entertaining this jolly crowd—and failed. She was not a social creature.

Walter decided to give Miss Pomeroy a Christmas present. What it would be, he could not imagine, for he had already given her the one good thing he owned—the picture of Abraham

Lincoln—and he had no access to real "presents." Then an idea came to him. He would create a present for Miss Pomeroy with his very own paws. He would paint a picture of himself!

That night, when Miss Pomeroy had read her book, turned out the bedside lamp, and fallen asleep, Walter hurried into her office. He took a piece of white typing paper and six Magic Markers and scurried down to his nest. He had a fragment of mirror there, which he used when he groomed himself, and this mirror would help him create the portrait.

Turning to the left and then to the right, Walter studied himself in the mirror. He was dismayed at how old he looked—and how white his muzzle had become—but his profile was still attractive and his whiskers were firm. For an old rat, he was not unbeautiful.

First he sketched himself with a stub of pencil. Then, when he was satisfied with the sketch, he began to fill it in with the colored pens. He cheated a little, by making his muzzle not as white as it really was, and by making his belly an unusual mauve. He colored his ears and nose pink. He colored his tail a gentle brown.

This endeavor took him all of one night, and most of the next. Around dawn he tiptoed into the backyard and picked some berries, which he Scotch-taped to his portrait by way of decoration. Using one of Miss Pomeroy's ballpoint pens, he wrote a greeting

at the bottom of
the picture. "Merry Christmas
from Walter," it said. "This is what I look like."

On Christmas Eve, the three churches in Safe Harbor rang
their bells. Far away there was the sound of human voices,
singing. Waiting until Miss Pomeroy was asleep, Walter hurried into her office—to leave his present for her on the desk.

There was a present there for *him*, a very small one. Astonished,
Walter picked it up and sniffed it. It was hard and square, and
wrapped in tissue paper. A tiny card attached to it said, "From
Amanda."

His paws trembling with excitement, Walter opened his
present. It was a very small, handmade book. The title on the
cover was *Walter: The Story of a Rat*.

The book was made out of the loveliest paper in the world, and

56

the text was in Miss Pomeroy's handwriting. The back and front covers were cardboard, and the pages had been sewn together with colored twine. Walter began to read.

The story was indeed about *him*—but because it was a fictional story, it was not exactly his life. But then, how could it be? Miss Pomeroy did not know his life. What she had chosen to write was a very clever piece about a rat who, after surviving many catastrophes, settles down in the house of a poet. The poet and the rat write verses for each other. Together, they write a book of poetry that wins an international prize.

What a moving story it was! And he, Walter, was the hero of it. Miss Pomeroy had portrayed him as both sensitive and brave, artistic and practical. Walter knew that for as long as he lived, he would treasure this book and keep it in a special place. In a way, he had now entered literary history, along with Kenneth Grahame's rat, and Oscar Wilde's.

He hurried downstairs toward his nest, wanting to put his present in a safe place. Passing through the kitchen, he discovered that he was hungry and decided to stop for a snack. There—on the kitchen counter—another present awaited him. It was a plate of treats, left there for him by Miss Pomeroy. Another card said, "Walter: Help yourself."

She had not done the conventional thing—which would have been to offer him cheese. Instead, the china plate held two

Christmas cookies, half a tangerine, some pieces of liverwurst, and a hardboiled egg. It was the finest meal Walter had ever eaten, and the most original. He put the plate in the sink afterward.

W alter slept late on Christmas morning, wakened only by the sound of birds in the backyard. Stretching, he untangled himself from his warm bed and looked for his book. It was right there, near the fragment of mirror, and he found it more wonderful than ever. Once again, he read the entire story. Once again, he marveled that he had become the hero of a book.

The weather outside looked unusually mild for December. It

was a day to sit on Miss Pomeroy's bench and appreciate the world. So, after grooming his fur and cleaning his whiskers, Walter exited from his nest into the sunny day.

In the garden another surprise awaited him—for Miss Pomeroy was there, on the stone bench, drinking a cup of coffee. She had her tweed overcoat on, and a long red scarf around her neck. Beneath the overcoat, Walter could see flannel pajamas.

He had never been this close to Miss Pomeroy before, and the closeness made him feel faint. How beautiful she was! Not beautiful in a conventional way, but in some way he could not define. Her brown hair, streaked with white, was both messy and attractive. Her eyes, as she gazed around the garden, were a startling blue.

Walter's heart was pounding so loudly that he was sure Miss Pomeroy could hear it. Every part of him twitched and trembled—and, when he thought about it later, reliving the moment, he would realize that the twitching and trembling were a kind of love.

What should he do? Approach her, or retreat back into his nest? Make some kind of sound—a careful squeak—or remain silent? If she saw him, would she scream and faint? No. It was not possible. They had exchanged Christmas gifts. She had made him the hero of a book.

Putting one paw after another in the most delicate way, Walter approached Miss Pomeroy. She glanced at him, nodded, and continued to peruse the garden. Emboldened, Walter climbed up on the bench and sat at the farthest edge, glancing at Miss Pomeroy nervously. She was not alarmed. She was simply . . . herself.

Walter edged a little closer to Miss Pomeroy, and she shifted her weight slightly, making room for him. Finally, he was sitting quite close to her, almost touching, as the two of them looked out at the winter world.

They stayed that way for a long time—two friends on a bench in the middle of winter. A writer and a reader, a person and a rat. And after about an hour, when the weather turned cold, they went back into the house together.